For my boys Harry, Charlie, Billy and Max

InvestDev Books

The Magic Trampoline

Copyright © Kieren J Fitz-Gibbon, 2017

Illustrations by Danh Tran Art

First published 2017

Email: adventure@themagictrampoline.com

www.themagictrampoline.com

The Magic Trampoline

ISBN 978-0-646-99536-6

Printed in Australia

987654321

The Magic Trampoline

An original adventure series by Kieren J. Fitz-Gibbon

Imagine what could happen if you jumped too high on your trampoline. If the Magic Trampoline comes to your house you may find out!

Come along with Haz, Chaz, Baz, and Maz as they use the magic trampoline to travel to amazing places and have great adventures.

The best part is, they always get home safely…and Mum never finds out.

It was a loud, almost deafening thunderstorm.

A flash of light…and something magical happened.

What adventure would be waiting for the boys the next day?

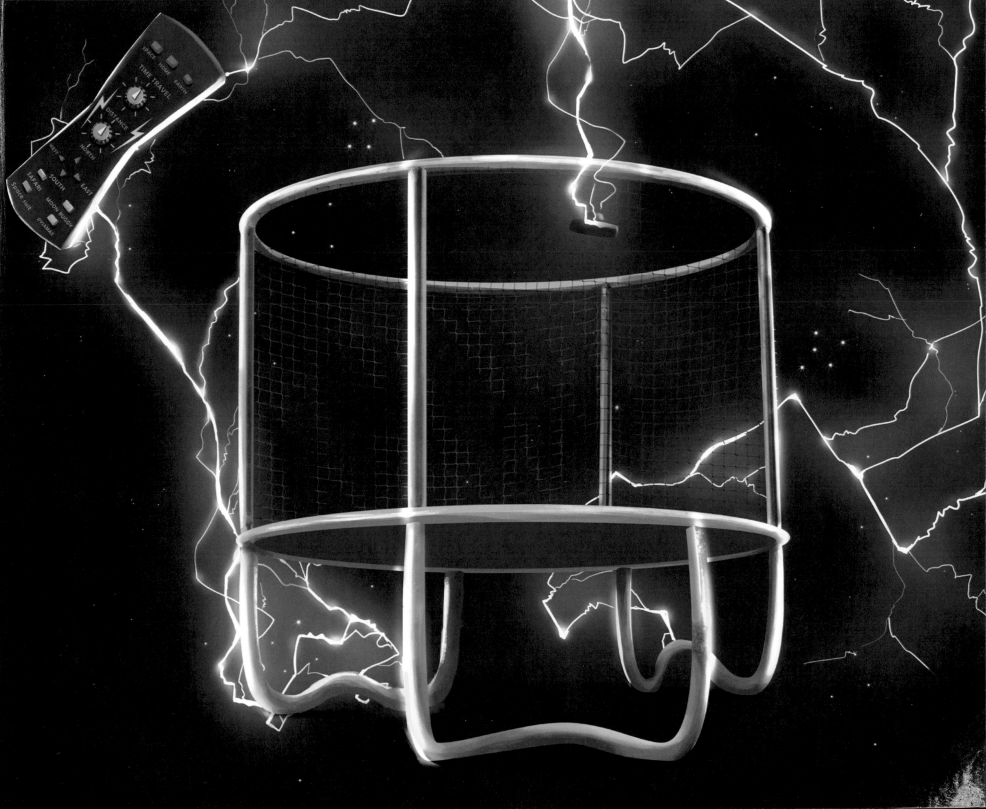

Like erupting volcanos, three brothers - Haz, Chaz and Baz sprang out of bed.

"Time to wake Dad up," Chaz declared.

"DAD! DAD! Get up!" shouted all three.

They yanked Dad's feet, pulled his arms, and jumped madly up and down on the bed. Maz the baby just giggled watching his crazy brothers.

"DAD, can we go outside and play?" Chaz asked loudly.

Dad fell out of bed with a THUD! "Okay boys," he groaned.

Mum rolled over and went back to sleep.

The boys raced outside to their trusty trampoline. They climbed up and bounced.

Baz, the youngest of the three, spotted a switch on the inside of the net—the boys had never seen it before.

"What's that?" he pointed curiously.

"Leave it alone, Baz – don't touch it," Haz yelled.

Too late!

"Nooooo," Haz cried, "I said DON'T touch it!"

The trampoline wobbled, colours swirled, stars appeared and twinkled around them…

"What's going on?" Chaz cried out.

There was no time for an answer.

The three bouncing boys launched like rockets into the air!

Up, up, up they went, over the house, through the clouds, higher and higher into the sky. Then they stopped going up!

Down, down, down they fell, faster and faster, tumbling toward the ground.

The boys weren't scared – they were flying, and they loved every minute of it.

They spotted the trampoline in their yard and started to slow down.

Slower and slower, lower and lower until they landed, and kept on bouncing as if nothing had happened!

The three brothers looked at each other in amazement.

"Let's get Dad," Chaz shouted. "DAAAD! Come outside, quickly!"

"What is it, Chaz?" Dad answered.

"Our trampoline just bounced us into the sky!" Chaz panted.

"Unbelievable!" Dad yelled back, then out he ran waving a twinkling, buzzing and sparkly remote control!

Everyone walked nervously toward the trampoline. They climbed up. They jumped.

"Hit the switch Baz," Haz said excitedly.

The trampoline wobbled, colours swirled, stars appeared and twinkled around them.

The bouncing boys and Dad and Maz, launched like rockets into the air!

Up, up, up they went, over the house, through the clouds, higher and higher into the sky. Before they knew it they were blasting into space!

"We need space suits!" Dad shouted. He pushed a button on the remote control.

The little astronauts roared past Mars, Saturn and Neptune. They waved to the International Space Station!

They were headed towards the smallest planet in the universe – Planet Tiny!

As they approached, they saw something incredible. Their trampoline was waiting for them!

"DAD," the boys cried, "it is MAGIC!"

Slower and slower, lower and lower until they landed, and kept on bouncing as if nothing had happened!

They stepped off to explore.

Chaz heard some murmuring coming from behind a large rock.

"What was that?" he whispered, peeking out from behind Haz, his heart racing.

Out came a tiny alien. She had four arms, three legs, two tails, a head as big as her body, and a face as red as a tomato.

"Hello, I am Misty," the tiny alien said. "I am a friend. Who are you?"

"Hi Misty, I'm Haz. This is Chaz, Baz, Maz, and our dad," Haz replied. "We are from Planet Earth."

"Earthlings! Come, come and meet my friends."

Three more aliens just like Misty peered out from behind the rocks.

"This is Merlee, Fizz, and Krick," Misty introduced them. "We love visitors! We like to play games," she said. "Will you play with us?"

"Yes!" The boys shouted together.

"Let's play soccer!" Haz hollered. He loved to score goals.

The crowd of boys and their newfound friends set off to the alien soccer field.

It was humans versus aliens. The aliens were excellent soccer players, after all, they did have three legs!

There were lots of goals scored and even more high fives!

After what seemed like hours of wonderful fun, everyone collapsed exhausted.

It had been the most fantastic game of intergalactic soccer ever played.

"It's time to go home," Dad said sadly.

The magic trampoline appeared in front of the goals.

As they said their goodbyes and promised to return, no-one but Maz noticed Misty sneaking into Dad's backpack. Maz just smiled and kept Misty's secret.

The boys climbed aboard and Haz hit the switch.

The trampoline wobbled, colours swirled, stars appeared and twinkled around them… they rocketed back into space.

As Earth approached, they saw their home and spotted their trampoline.

Slower and slower, lower and lower…

Poking out of Dad's backpack was a blue and yellow tail!

"Umm… I think we have a problem guys," Chaz announced.

Misty stuck her head out. "SURPRISE!" she yelled.

"OH NO! We have to hide her before Mum finds out," Haz said worriedly. Mum didn't like animals in the house, let alone aliens!

"Where can we hide her?" Baz asked frantically.

"Inside?" Chaz suggested.

They raced noisily to the boys' bedroom. Misty scrambled under the bed just in time!

Mum opened the door…

"What are you boys up to?" Mum asked.

"Nothing," they answered.

Misty's tail poked out from beside the bed…luckily Mum didn't see it. Mum didn't even hear the soft alien giggle coming from under the bed as she left.

The boys looked at each other with disbelief in their eyes.

How were they going to get Misty back home? What would happen if Mum found her?

Well, that's a story for another day…

…to be continued